I am **Ook, Ook** the **book.**
Will you stop and take a look?
You will see, I'm one good **book!**

Meet **Ug the Bug, Ee the Bee, Ing the Thing** and a parade of nine other zany characters. With its fun, tongue-twisting rhymes and witty illustrations, *Ook the Book* will have readers in stitches, while slyly introducing them to some of the fundamental sounds of the language. A perfect book for budding bookworms!

"A useful and fun addition to easy-reader shelves."
—*School Library Journal*

". . . catchy. . . . an unstoppable word game."
—*Publishers Weekly*

pet

Net

wet

cow

bow wow wow

squid

Look

book

Nook

Glug

hug

cat

Lin

pin

twin

beep

Peep

jeep

Sid

bee

tree

Lake

bake

cake

rat

fly

cry

string

ring

king

For Kia and Niko who helped me with every last word. —L. R.

For David —S. M.

First paperback edition published in 2006 by Chronicle Books LLC.

Text © 2001 by Lissa Rovetch.
Illustrations © 2001 by Shannon McNeill.

Book design by Paul Donald | Graphic Detail.
Typeset in Geometric 415.
The illustrations in this book were rendered in gouache and black ink.
Manufactured in Hong Kong.
ISBN-10 0-8118-5029-3
ISBN-13 978-0-8118-5029-2

The Library of Congress has catalogued the previous edition as follows:
Rovetch, Lissa.
Ook the Book / by Lissa Rovetch ; illustrated by Shannon McNeill.
p. cm.
Summary: A collection of twelve humorous rhymes designed to help new readers become familiar with both the appearance and sound of written and spoken English.
ISBN 0-8118-2660-0
1. English language—Vowels—Juvenile literature. 2. English language—Phonetics—Juvenile literature.
    [1. English language—Phonetics.] 1. McNeill, Shannon, 1970- ill. II. Title
PE1157.R65 2001
428.1—dc21
00-008942

Distributed in Canada by Raincoast Books
9050 Shaughnessy Street, Vancouver, British Columbia V6P 6E5

10 9 8 7 6 5 4 3 2 1

Chronicle Books LLC
85 Second Street, San Francisco, California 94105

www.chroniclekids.com

Ook the Book

by Lissa Rovetch

illustrated by
Shannon McNeill

chronicle books · san francisco

I am **Ook**,
Ook the **book**.

Do you see me
in my **nook**?

Will you stop
and take a **look**?

You will see,
I'm one good **book**!

I am Ake,

Ake the snake.

I can bake. See my cake?

If you take my snake cake,

I will put you in the lake!

Do you want a **bug slug hug**?

I am At,
At the cat.

Do you see Pat?
He is my rat.

I sat on Pat,
so he is flat.

WELCOME

I am **Et**,

Et the **pet**.

Et the **wet pet** in a **net**.

Do you need a **wet net pet?**

You can **get**

me free I **bet**.

Ee the Bee

I am Ee,
Ee the bee.

Do you see Lee,
up in the tree?

You are **free** to look for **Lee.**

But **gee,** that **bee** is hard to **see!**

I am **Eep**,
Eep the **sheep**.
This is **Peep**.
She needs to **sleep**.
Please do not
make that **jeep**

go **beep!**

ID the Kid

I am Id, Id the kid.

Did you see what I just did?

I hid a squid under old Sid!

I am Ing,
Ing the thing.
I bring string
to the king.
If you need
a bit of string,
just give a ring,
to Ing the thing.

Ow the Cow

I am **Ow**,
Ow the **cow**.
I can bark. **Bow wow wow.**
Don't ask me why,
don't ask me **how.**
I am just that kind
of **cow.**

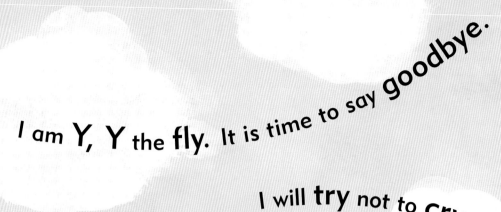

I am **Y, Y** the **fly.** It is time to say **goodbye.**

I will **try** not to **cry.**

But **my,** it's hard to say **goodbye!**

pet

Net

wet

cow

bow wow wow

squid

Look

book

Nook

Glug

hug

cat

Lin

pin

twin